"Caitlin's Wish is an imaginative book, beautifully illustrated that can be a fun family read and a terrific resource in schools and youth settings to ensure that all young people have a better understanding of the road travelled by young people with caring responsibilities. Crossroads Care is delighted to be linked to this publication and would encourage everyone to buy their own copy and then get one to pass on to friends and family"

GOFAL CROES FFYRDD
CROSS ROADS CARE

Angela Roberts. Director for Crossroads Care, Wales, UK

"What happens when a parent becomes ill? Victoria Taylor has taken her own family's experiences with chronic Intracranial Hypertension (IH) and written an imaginative tale with love, insight, and gentle reassurance. Caitlin's Wish is a delight to read and look at, with watercolour illustrations of a magical world. It helps families and educators navigate the uncertainty of chronic illness and guide children in a creative and loving way. Add Caitlin's Wish to your gift list; it should be part of every child's library."

Emanuel Tanne, M.D. Co-Founder and President of the Intracranial Hypertension Research Foundation.

"Caitlin's Wish is an imaginative, thought provoking book which is beautifully illustrated. It makes a perfect resource for schools to use in conjunction with the 'Princess Royal Trust for Carers' schools resource pack.' Reading Caitlin's Wish will enable young people to gain a better understanding of what being a young carer is really like. Furthermore reading it will encourage greater empathy, respect and tolerance from all ages who are not personally affected by illness or disability themselves.

I am delighted to say that Neath Port Talbot County Borough Council has ordered copies of this book for circulation in its libraries and schools."

Karl Napieralla OBE, Director of Education, Leisure and Life long Learning, Neath Port Talbot, Wales, UK.

"Caitlin's Wish is an enchanting and very moving story which really engages the reader and is appealing on many different levels. It is a good starting point for discussion with older children on the topics of having an optimistic outlook on illness and disability within the family and of course being a young carer. For young carers or those living at home with a disabled person it highlights that they are not alone, other families face similar situations. Equally, it is a lovely gentle tale to have read out loud at story time to younger children who will enjoy the colourful illustrations. Children of all ages who hear or read this story will remember it and the messages it conveys for a very long time.

The Neath Port Talbot Young Carers Forum which is made up of representatives from agencies that are concerned with the issues facing young carers and their families, whole heartedly supports Caitlin's Wish as a resource that raises awareness of the needs of young carers and issues of disability."
Neath Port Talbot Young Carers Forum.

"Seeing someone become ill, whom you love dearly, can be extremely frightening, sad, painful and very confusing. It is even harder if you are a child. There are so few resources available that give a true life reflection of how it feels to become a young carer, and how this impacts on your daily life, and changes everything, often for ever. Young Carers feel unable to talk to those that they are close to, for fear of causing further pain and upset. However, it is vital that Young Carers can talk openly; understand that they are not alone, and most importantly be given support to know they are not to blame for the illness of their loved ones. Caitlins Wish' is an imaginative, clever, honest and beautiful story that addresses these issues. It gives a strong, clear and supportive message to young carers, whilst assisting and teaching them to understand the true implications of their role, and the impact of the illness on their family. It is an inspirational read, that must be made available to Young carers of all ages. A truly remarkable story."
Sonia Binge, Senior Social Work Manager, Children with Disabilities service, Berkshire, England, UK.

"This is a very meaningful and enchanting book. It is an inspiration to young carers all over the world. I like the way that reality is mixed with a fairytale of outstanding wonder and hope. Thank you for writing this book, if I could rate it, it would be five stars."
Adele Taylor. Age 11. Swansea, Neath Port Talbot Crossroads Young Carers Project, Wales, UK.

"The book is a very insightful journey into the mind of a young carer trying to come to terms with illness. A magical adventure."
Chris Taylor. Age 14. Swansea, Neath Port Talbot Crossroads Young Carers Project, Wales, UK.

"I loved the book. I can really relate to it with my Mom being sick too. It is a great way to let other kids know what it is like to have a parent who is sick all the time."
Teraesa, Aged 11. Young Carer, Texas, USA

"This book is beautifully written. It does a great job of showing what life is like for young carers and helps children realize that they are not alone in the way that they feel. I definitely recommend it to any child who is faced with watching their loved ones battle an illness."
"Victoria Taylor puts an enchanting twist on how to stay positive in times of hardship. People of all ages can learn a valuable lesson from reading Caitlin's Wish."
Kayla Jackson, Aged 17. Young Carer, Indiana, USA

"I really enjoyed Caitlin's Wish; it was a really good way to raise awareness of IH and young carers. It's helpful to young carers because it helps you to understand you're not alone."
Jaimie. Aged 12. Swansea, Neath Port Talbot Crossroads Young Carers Project, Wales, UK.

"I think families should read this book together. These types of topics are so hard to talk about, especially for children. This book opens the dialogue and helps everyone so much. Caitlin's Wish has given me the perspective I needed to keep positive, both for myself and those around me. Thank you Victoria for telling a beautiful story that can teach us all a little about coping with life altering illness and making the best out of the life you are given."
Brittany Hazelton, California, USA.
www.youtube.com/brittydragon

"I loved how this book was easy for kids with parents who have IH to relate to. I'm excited to see how it spreads the word about IH."
Dona, Aged 13, Young Carer, Texas, USA.

"The book is really good, I would have found this story really helpful when I was younger and I think it's great for the 'younger' young carers. I really like all the pictures and fairies too!"
Lauren. Aged 14. Swansea, Neath Port Talbot Crossroads Young Carers Project, Wales, UK.

"I could relate to the book with the Dad being sick and sleeping all the time, it's the same with my Mom - especially with her headaches."
Jakob, Age 12. Young Carer, Texas, USA

"I really enjoyed reading Caitlin's Wish; it is a really good story. It raises awareness and shows other people what a young carer really does. It's helpful because not many people know what a young carer is."
Laura. Aged 13. Swansea, Neath Port Talbot Crossroads Young Carers Project

"Caitlin's Wish has changed our lives forever. When I was diagnosed with IH in 2008, our daughter Bella remained cheerful and positive; however, there was always a little less sparkle in her eye. She now knows she is not alone and there are many other children that she has so much in common with. Thank you Victoria, from our family to you for putting the sparkle back in our daughter's eyes! Much love and thanks forever!"
Robin Cline Phillips, California, USA

"As a Mom with IH, I greatly appreciate what Caitlin's Wish gives to our children. It gives them a way to escape the stress that comes along with having an ill parent. Thank you for giving this wonderful gift to our children and for raising more awareness of Intracranial Hypertension."
Brooke Pettigrew, Texas, USA

Caitlin's Wish

Second Edition

VICTORIA TAYLOR

ILLUSTRATED BY CLAIRE WILES

Matador
9 Priory Business Park
Kibworth Beauchamp
Leicester LE8 0RX, UK
Tel: (+44) 116 279 2299
Fax: (+44) 116 279 2277
Email: books@troubador.co.uk
Web: www.troubador.co.uk/matador

ISBN 978 1780881 010

British Library Cataloguing in Publication Data.
A catalogue record for this book is available from the British Library.

Typeset by Troubador Publishing Ltd, Leicester, UK

Matador is an imprint of Troubador Publishing Ltd

For

Adele and Chris

With Love

Contents

INTRODUCTION

Caitlin's Wish is based on a true story.

Victoria had been happily married for 7 years when her husband was diagnosed with a rare brain condition called I.H.* (or Pseudotumour Cerebri.)

He had to retire from his teaching career as a result of ill health. Their children were very young when he was diagnosed; just 6 years old and 2 years old.

Initially the children coped well with all the changes in their lives. Their eldest child could remember his father before IH and so he had more patience and sympathy for him. He describes it as having had two Dads – the one before IH, and the one with IH.

Photograph by www.phrphotography.com

Their youngest child was so young that she just accepted the situation. It was only when she started school that she realised her life was different. She felt confused, sad, angry and isolated. Her friends were too young to understand what her life as a young carer was like, let alone how she felt. Just like Caitlin in the story, she felt as if no-one understood.

At the age of 6 years old, she was too young to access any of the local support networks for young carers. Victoria searched for books to help her daughter feel more positive about her situation, but couldn't find anything suitable at the time. In desperation she decided to write something and the idea behind Caitlin's Wish was born! The book helped her daughter so much that Victoria decided to publish it.

Victoria hopes that by reading 'Caitlin's Wish' children will learn to draw strength from the positive elements in their lives instead of dwelling on the negative; seeing what the sick/disabled person CAN do, instead of only seeing what they can't do any more. The book is also designed to help those who are not personally affected by illness or disability to gain an insight into how a young carer feels.

Victoria adds "It is hard to learn to live with a chronic illness or disability. You don't want your life to change, but you have no choice in the matter. You feel angry that it's happened to you. It's extremely difficult to let go of the life you had before. It seems so unfair! Why me? Why my family? It took us a long time to accept that we couldn't change anything, so we had to make the best of the situation. Through learning more about my husband's condition and how best to manage it, we slowly rebuilt our lives. We realised that we had to be open and honest with each other, always discussing things as a family. By focusing on the positive aspects in our lives it enabled us

to cope with the negative more easily.

The First Edition was published in 2010 and it soon became apparent that the book was being read by all ages, not just by younger children as it had been originally intended. Whole families were using the book to open the discussions into their own personal situations.

This Second Edition has been rewritten, taking into consideration all the book reviews and readers comments from the past 18 months.
This book is for all ages and it's envisaged that younger children will have it read to them.
Thank you for reading Caitlin's Wish. I hope it helps!"

Victoria Taylor

** For more information on IH please go to the IH Research Foundation's website – **www.ihrfoundation.org** **

CHAPTER ONE

Home Sweet Home

Our story begins in a beautiful little village, set deep in the heart of the Welsh countryside. It was a friendly place where everyone knew each other. It was a very old village made up of narrow winding lanes filled with quaint stone cottages, a village store and a church that was over two hundred years old. Most of the cottages still had thatched roofs, thick stone walls and roaring log fires that kept you snug and warm on a cold winter's night.

Down the lane behind the cottages was a large meadow which led onto the mountainside. It was covered with beautiful wild flowers, which were all the colours of the rainbow. This was where the village children would spend their days, running through the long grass and playing games together.

Alongside the meadow there was a shallow stream, with crystal clear water that ran down from the mountain. If you looked closely you could see different kinds of wildlife living in the stream, from fish darting in and out under the pebbles to frogs sitting on the rocks. Sometimes you could even catch a glimpse of kingfishers flying upstream, with their vivid electric blue colours flashing past. During the summer the children would sit by the stream, dipping their toes into the cool, clear water as they enjoyed the warm sunshine.

One such child was a little girl called Caitlin. She was small for her age, with pretty hazel green eyes and beautiful brown hair which fell across her face, so she could hide behind it if she wanted to. She was known for her radiant smile and wicked sense of humour. She was always cheery and could make even the grumpiest person smile. Caitlin's big brother was called Chris. He had bright blue eyes and short blond hair which spiked up on top of his head. Caitlin used to tease him, saying his hair was as spiky as a hedgehog.

They were the best of friends, as well as being brother and sister.

Caitlin had a special little friend called Rufus, but he wasn't a boy. Oh no, Rufus was actually a cheeky little robin. Caitlin had fed him every single day since he was very small and over time he had learned to trust her.

Everyday he would sit on her windowsill and listen carefully while she told him all about her day. He never answered back though, after all robins can't talk, can they?

Caitlin and Chris's Mother worked as a childminder during the week, so the house was always filled with fun and laughter. It was a great place to be! They had lots of fun playing games with the other children and they absolutely loved it.

Their Father worked away from home during the week, but once the weekend arrived he spent all his time with the family.

If the weather was nice, they would go on camping trips in the mountains. They'd spend their days lazing by the river catching fish, or cycling through the countryside. Sometimes they'd even go on boating trips across the mountain lakes or canoeing down the fast flowing rivers, it was so much fun.

In the evenings they'd sit around the campfire, toasting marshmallows and telling stories as the sun set in the distance. Chris excelled at storytelling. His stories were so funny; he had everyone hanging on his every word, waiting to hear what happened next.

Caitlin would make up songs and put on a show for everyone, she was such a talented entertainer. Mum and Dad would watch their children with beaming smiles on their faces; they were so proud of them.

If the family didn't go away for the weekend then their Father would take them on adventures closer to home, exploring the woodlands and forests that surrounded their village. He loved teaching the children all about the wildlife that lived nearby. One such time springs to mind.

CHAPTER TWO

Dad's Adventure

It was a beautiful day.

The April sunshine streamed through the kitchen window, shining across the table where Chris and Caitlin sat doing their homework. Their Father sat next to them, ready and willing to help whenever they needed him. Finally as they finished their homework Chris sat back in his chair and sighed "Thank goodness that's over and done with." He enjoyed studying, but not when the sun was shining.

Dad looked at him and smiled. "OK then, who wants to go on an adventure,"

"Ooh me, me, me" replied the children excitedly.

Mum was baking cakes in the kitchen, she turned and smiled, "Go on then, off you go. It'll be a while before I'm finished here."

The children ran over to their Mother and flung their arms around her, "Thanks Mum" they said.

Mum bent down and hugged them both tightly.

"Go on, have a good time, and be good!" she said.

"Right then, go and put your boots on" said Dad.

"Where are we going?" they asked.

"You'll find out in a minute" replied Dad.

They put their boots on quickly and were out of the door in a flash. Each linked arms with their father and chattered merrily as they walked along the old cart road into the forest.

"I know, let's play a game" said Dad.

"Let's see who can find clues to guess which animals live in the forest."

"Oh yes!" said Caitlin. "I can see a clue" she shouted, jumping up and down excitedly. "Look over there! I can see rabbit holes; that means that rabbits live here."

"Well aren't you clever?" said Dad, "You're right! Look over there Chris, can you see them?"

"Oh yes! Well done Caitlin."

As they walked further into the forest Chris suddenly covered his nose, pulling a face he asked "Urghh! What's that smell? It stinks!"

Dad burst out laughing. "That's a fox smell. They mark their territory with their scent."

"Urghh that's revolting!" said Chris.

"That's nature" said Dad, still laughing. "I know, why don't we go and have a look in the pond?"

They turned off the old cart road and started to walk across the meadow.

"Ah, I never get tired of this view" said Dad as he looked across at the mountains in the distance. "We're so lucky to live in such a beautiful area."

"Yes we are, it's lovely isn't it?" said Chris.

The April sunshine felt warm as they walked along, the only sounds they could hear were the birds singing sweetly in the trees. Nature was finally waking up again after the long winter. The meadow was covered with beautiful spring flowers, gently swaying in the breeze. As they reached the edge of the meadow they climbed over the wooden gate, jumped down onto the path and started walking across the mountain towards the pond.

"How far is it Daddy?" asked Caitlin.

"Oh not far" replied Dad.

As they walked along they could hear an unusual birdsong.

"What's that?" asked Caitlin.

"That's the first cuckoo of the spring!" said Dad excitedly. "Did you know that they fly all the way to Africa during the winter, because it's too cold for them here and in the spring they fly back again?"

"Wow! They're so clever!" said Caitlin.

Dad smiled at Caitlin, he loved sharing his knowledge of wildlife with his children.

As they got closer to the pond they could see dragonflies skating across the top of the water.

"Look!" said Dad "they look like fairies dancing."

"Don't be so silly Daddy, they are dragon flies" stated Caitlin with her hands on her hips. "Anyway fairies don't exist!"

"Shh!" said Dad quickly "fairies are real, and they can hear you! You'll upset them if you're not careful."

Caitlin looked down at the floor, she didn't want to argue with her father, but she didn't believe him.

"Come on, we'll sit over there" said Dad pointing to a grassy bank. Caitlin went and sat under a nearby tree sulking. She hated it when her father corrected her, but she still didn't believe in fairies no matter what he said.

"Oh come on Caitlin, stop sulking" said Dad. He went over to her and gave her a hug. "One day you'll understand all about fairies, but in the meantime if you don't believe in them then that's alright, just don't say it out loud, OK?"

"OK Daddy" said Caitlin hugging her father. She didn't want to spoil the outing, but she felt that she had to get her point across; after all she wasn't a baby anymore.

"Now we have to sit still and be very quiet" explained Dad.

They didn't have to wait long before they saw brown speckled fish swimming in the water.

"Wow!" whispered Caitlin. Just then she heard a popping sound coming from the water. She looked around to see what it was. It looked like a baby lizard. "What's that?" she asked.

"That's a newt" said Dad. "The popping sound you heard was it coming up out of the water to breathe."

"I didn't know that there were funny looking lizards living so close to my house!" said Caitlin. She felt very uncomfortable with this thought. "What if they decide to go for a walk to our house and they climb in through my bedroom window?" She shivered at the thought.

"Oh don't be silly Caitlin" said Dad giving her a cuddle to reassure her.

"They need to stay near the water. They're not going to venture as far as our house." Dad smiled "You silly Billy Tillie!"

He knew that this always made her smile, and it

worked again this time. She looked up at her father with a half smile "Are you absolutely sure they won't walk to my house?"

"I'm sure sweetheart. Don't worry."

Just then Chris pointed across the pond "Look!" he said "there's a frog sitting over there on the rocks."

Suddenly the frog jumped into the water and disappeared from view, at the same time the fish and the newt swam under the rocks out of sight. "Where did they go, Dad?" asked Chris.

"I don't know" replied Dad. Just then they all saw a large bird swooping towards them. Caitlin ducked, putting her hands across her head in fear.

"Don't worry Caitlin, that's a heron. He won't hurt you, but now we know why they all disappeared so quickly. Herons like to eat frogs, and fish, and …."

"Newts" said Chris smiling "Thank goodness they managed to hide in time."

"Exactly" replied Dad "they must have seen him. Now that they're all hiding from the heron we might as well head back home. They won't come out again for ages."

"OK Dad"

When they reached the meadow Dad suggested that they walk alongside the stream. "Who knows, we might see some more wildlife" he said.

Caitlin saw little holes in the bank which she hadn't noticed before. "What are those?" she asked, pointing towards them.

"They're birds' nests Caitlin, probably robins' nests."

Caitlin gazed in wonder. "Maybe Rufus lives there" she thought to herself.

As they walked along Dad suddenly had an idea. "I know, let's pick some flowers for Mum, shall we?"

"Oh yes!" said the children. They loved surprising their Mother with flowers. Each darted off in different directions to search for Mum's favourite flowers. Mum was thrilled when they gave them to her.

"They're so beautiful, and look; you found my favourite flowers as well. Thank you so much."
They took pride of place on the kitchen windowsill.

So as you can see, life was sweet for Caitlin and Chris.

Little did they know, all that was about to change.

CHAPTER THREE

Caitlin's Lost Smile.

It started slowly, with Dad being ill when he came home at the weekends. Everyone just thought that he'd been working too hard. Dad didn't have the energy to do anything anymore. He spent most of his time in bed. Eventually he became so poorly that he was rushed into hospital.

Chris and Caitlin were frightened. They'd never seen him like this before. They felt completely helpless. Mum tried to be strong; protecting them from what was happening, but it was no use. They knew that whatever was wrong with Daddy, it was serious. It was impossible to hide that from them.

A million questions raced through their young minds. "What if the Doctors couldn't find out what was wrong with him? Was Daddy going to die? What would happen if he did?"

Even the thought of losing him was too much to bear. They both adored him.

The Doctor asked Mum to go into his office. "Wait here while I go and talk to the Doctor" she said to the children, pointing to two chairs in the hospital corridor. "I won't be long."

She must have only been gone for about 20 minutes, but it felt like an eternity to the children. As she came out of the room she beckoned to them "Come over here and sit down. I want to talk to you."

Caitlin jumped onto her mother's lap and Chris sat beside them.

"Now you know that Daddy is very poorly, don't you?"

"Yes" they both replied.

"Well the Doctors are going to have to do lots of different tests to figure out what's wrong with him. That means he's going to have to stay in hospital for a little while."

Chris and Caitlin began to cry.
They didn't want Daddy to stay in hospital. Mum put her arms around them reassuringly; it worried her to see them so distressed.

"Hey, come on. It'll be OK" she said, trying to remain optimistic.
"I've just spoken to your Grandma and Granddad and they're on their way. They'll take you home and look after you while I stay here with Daddy."

"But Mummy, I don't want to go home and leave you here" said Caitlin clinging to her mother.

"Don't worry sweetheart, I'll be home later on to tuck you into bed."

"You promise?"

"I promise darling."

"When will we see Daddy though?" she asked.

"Grandma and Granddad will bring you to see him every day after school, OK?"

Caitlin nodded her head. "OK" she said reluctantly.

Mum turned to Chris. "I need you to be a big boy for me now. Be strong, and help your Grandma and Granddad with Caitlin. Can you do that for me sweetheart?"

"Yes" said Chris wiping a tear from his eye. "I love you Mum" he whispered as he hugged her tightly.

"And I love you too."

Mum turned to Caitlin "I love you my little princess."

"I love you too Mummy" said Caitlin hugging her tightly, not wanting to let go.

Grandma and Granddad arrived soon after and took the children home.

Later that same evening after Caitlin had gone to bed, Chris decided to ask his Grandma a question that was bothering him. He sat beside her in front of the fire. "Can I please ask you something, Grandma?" he said nervously.

"Yes dear, what's the matter?"

Chris couldn't hold back the tears as he spoke "Oh Grandma, what will we do if Daddy dies? I couldn't bear it if anything happened to him."

Grandma put her arms around Chris and rocked him gently, just as she had when he was a baby. He was trembling from head to toe; completely terrified of the thoughts that had been going around inside his head all day.

"I know this is all very scary, but it's going to be OK, sweetheart. I'm sure that the Doctors will find out what's wrong with him. We have to have faith Chris. I'm sure he'll be home again before you know it."

"Do you really think so?" asked Chris.

"Yes my darling, I do. Please don't worry. Everything's going to be alright."

As it turned out Grandma was right. Dad was in hospital for a while but eventually the Doctors worked out what was wrong with him. He had a rare illness that caused horrible symptoms. He was too ill to work anymore and he was in pain most of the time. Mum had to give up work to look after Dad and everything in Chris and Caitlin's lives changed.

It was such a confusing time for everyone; their lives were changing before their eyes and there was absolutely nothing they could do to stop it. They were relieved that Daddy was home, yet at the same time they were sad that he couldn't do all the things that he used to be able to do. The whole family felt angry.

"Why us?" they'd say. "Life's not fair!"

Chris and Caitlin became inseparable; leaning on each other for support. They both thought that no-one else could possibly understand how they felt.

Mum spent a lot of time talking things through with them. She explained that Dad was always in pain, but that he had good days and bad days. She explained that Dad wouldn't die from this illness, but he would be poorly from now on.

Whenever Dad had a good day he would make the most of being in less pain and they would go on a family outing together. The children treasured these moments dearly. However on the bad days Dad would sleep nearly all day. The children had to be quiet so as not to disturb him, which made life miserable.

Each child coped differently.

Chris found it easier to adjust than Caitlin. He had always been the quieter child anyway. He enjoyed reading and drawing, whereas Caitlin was a bubbly personality who would sing at the top of her voice all day long. She could still be noisy outside, but she couldn't be noisy inside the cottage anymore. This was really strange for Caitlin; with Mum having been a childminder the house had always been noisy, very noisy with lots of children running around. Now it had to be quiet.

IT WAS TOO QUIET!

Caitlin hated it! She felt so angry; she wanted to scream 'WHY ME?'

Everything seemed so hopeless; she felt as if she was in a nightmare that she couldn't wake up from.

Occasionally Mum would pause to reflect how their lives had changed. She felt heartbroken that her children weren't getting the childhood she'd imagined they'd have, and she'd have a little cry to herself. Caitlin had an uncanny knack of walking into the room at this point. It upset her to see her Mum crying, especially as she was such a tower of strength for the children. Caitlin would wipe away her Mother's tears and give her a hug to comfort her.

Caitlin didn't tell anyone how she really felt, apart from Rufus. She poured her heart out to him. She trusted him. But what could he do? He was just a little robin. He couldn't change anything, could he? Her smile was definitely lost. That radiant beaming smile that had always been a ray of sunshine was gone. She couldn't think of anything she had to smile about. She had never felt so sad and alone. However Caitlin didn't know that by talking to Rufus, she was actually asking for help. She could never have imagined what was about to happen next.

CHAPTER FOUR

Bethan's Visit.

It was a cold November evening and the stars sparkled in the midnight blue sky. It was a beautiful night, yet Caitlin couldn't appreciate it because she was so sad. A large tear rolled down her cheek as she looked up to the moon.

"It's not fair! Why me? Why did it have to be MY Dad?" she sobbed. "Why can't life go back to how it was before? I hate this!"

She was angry that this had happened to her family and she couldn't understand why. The sad truth was that there was no reason why. It was nobody's fault, so there was no one to blame. Caitlin felt so lost and alone. She was totally unaware that Rufus (the robin) had been to see his friend Bethan and she had a plan!

Caitlin climbed into bed. As she snuggled down underneath her duvet, tears still rolling down her face, she noticed a bright light in the corner of the room. She quickly dried her eyes. She wanted to see what this strange light was.

As the light got bigger and bigger it started to look like….. An Angel!

"An Angel?" she thought. "No, it can't be. I must be dreaming!"

She rubbed her eyes hard and looked again. The Angel was still standing there, smiling at Caitlin. She glistened from head to toe; her bright blonde hair shimmered like gold and she had the most unusual deep brown eyes that seemed to soothe the soul. Caitlin was fascinated by her wings which were made out of soft, snow white feathers.

It was strange because she should have been scared, but she wasn't. In fact it was the opposite! She felt calm and tranquil; a feeling she hadn't experienced in a very long time.

"My dear child" said the Angel. "Your sadness has been heard in heaven and I have been sent to help you. My name is Bethan and I'm an Angel. I've come to take you to a magical place called Fairyland."

"What, now?"

"Yes, now Caitlin. Everyone is waiting for you."

"What do you mean 'everyone is waiting for me'?" asked Caitlin.

"The fairy folk are all waiting to help you in Fairyland" explained Bethan. "If you agree, we'll leave now and you'll be home again before anyone even notices you've gone."

Caitlin thought hard. What should she do? Her Mother had always taught her that she should never go anywhere with strangers, but did that include Angels and Fairies? Or maybe this was all a dream? So many questions whizzed around inside her head. She pinched herself hard. "Ouch!" she said. Well at least she knew that she wasn't dreaming. But what should she do?

Bethan picked up on what she was thinking and said "I know Mummy has said that you should never go anywhere with strangers, and she's absolutely right. She's teaching you to stay safe. This is different though. Caitlin I promise that you will be safe. Rufus has told me all about you."

"Wait a minute… Rufus?"

Caitlin looked confused. "But Rufus is a…"

"Robin. Yes I know Caitlin. All will become clear in time, don't worry" replied Bethan.

"We just want to help you. In Fairyland there's a special tree called the Healing Tree. Angels just like me take children there to help them see their lives differently."

"Can this Healing Tree really help me?" asked Caitlin. "I don't want to feel sad any more. I love my Daddy so much and I know that it's not his fault he's ill."

"Yes, the Healing Tree will definitely be able to help you Caitlin. You'll see things differently by the morning."

"You promise that I'll be back before anyone notices that I've gone?"

"Of course, I promise!" replied Bethan.

"OK then, let's go!" said Caitlin.

CHAPTER FIVE

Fairyland

The stars shimmered in the moonlit sky; sprinkling their stardust across the world. The air was filled with anticipation as Bethan took Caitlin's hand.

"Are you ready?" she asked.

"Yes, I am" said Caitlin.

The next thing she knew she was in the air, soaring high above the rooftops, flying through the night. The landscape looked so different, everything seemed so small.

"Chris would love this!" she thought to herself. "If only he could see me now."

"Hold my hand tightly. Don't let go!" warned Bethan.

"Oh I won't let go, don't worry" said Caitlin thinking to herself "Let go? It's a long way down if I do!"

Suddenly there was a flash of light that lit up the whole sky. Glittering sparks of gold, yellow and white lights surrounded Caitlin.

"Hold tight" shouted Bethan. "We're nearly there!"

Caitlin shut her eyes tight in fear. When she opened them she couldn't believe what she saw.

It was daytime in Fairyland. The sky was the most vivid blue she'd ever seen, with not a cloud in sight and the warm sun shone in the distance. They landed gently in beautiful woodland with grass so soft it felt like a carpet underneath Caitlin's feet. They were surrounded by brightly coloured flowers;

each one tiny yet perfectly formed. It was enchanting.

In the distance Caitlin could see a group of fairies sitting on the banks of a stream, each dipping their toes into the cool crystal clear water beneath them.

Caitlin stared at them in awe. They were breathtakingly beautiful. Their faces reminded Caitlin of her china dolls at home, so tiny and perfect in every way.

Each had long hair cascading in waves down their backs and they were dressed in the most unusual lilacs, pale rose pinks, bright yellows and deep cornflower blues that you could imagine. Their delicate wings matched the colour of their dresses, yet each time they fluttered all you could see were the shimmering silver edges sparkling in the sunshine.

Caitlin's heart skipped a beat as each fairy turned to wave and say hello to her.

"Hello" she replied smiling.

That smile which had been lost for so long was already back, and she'd only been in Fairyland for a few minutes.

Just then Caitlin heard giggling coming from the dense woodland which surrounded her. She looked around to see where the sound was coming from. Suddenly she saw pixies chasing each other in and out of the trees. She gasped in shock putting her hands to her mouth.

"Are you alright?" asked Bethan.

"Yes" replied Caitlin "It's just a bit overwhelming. I didn't think fairies and pixies were real until tonight. I just thought that they were characters in books until now. The fairies were absolutely beautiful and now I have seen pixies for the first time as well. They aren't how I imagined they'd be at all." The pixies overheard Caitlin talking and decided to come and introduce themselves properly.

There were 3 in total, each dressed in little outfits made from oak leaves, with leaf shaped hats on their heads. They had piercing dark brown eyes, a cute little pointed nose and long pointy ears that stuck out of the sides of their hats.

Each pixie stepped towards Caitlin in turn holding out their hand to shake hands with her. They each bowed their heads as they greeted her.

"Welcome Miss Caitlin" they said politely. "We are very pleased to meet you."

"Thank you" said Caitlin shaking their hands. Her smile now stretched from ear to ear as she felt the anticipation in the air. She was so excited.

"Goodbye Miss Caitlin" said the pixies as they ran back into the woodlands to carry on with their game.

"Goodbye" said Caitlin.

As Caitlin turned around she saw an unusual narrow winding pathway. It led into the woodland, disappearing out of sight amongst the trees. It wasn't just any path though; it was made from dusty pink earth with green plants growing through it.

Caitlin didn't question it though; she was quickly learning to expect the unexpected here; after all it was Fairyland!

"Bethan, where does that pathway go?" she asked.

"You'll see. Come on! Let's go to the Healing Tree."

As they began to walk along the path Caitlin said "It's so peaceful here. Everyone is so friendly. Thank you for bringing me to Fairyland, I feel so much happier already and we haven't even got to the Healing Tree yet."

"Now do you see why I wanted to bring you here?" asked Bethan.

"Oh yes, I understand. Thank you!" said Caitlin.

CHAPTER SIX

The Healing Tree

As they turned the corner they found themselves in a beautiful clearing. In the middle of the clearing there stood a very old tree. Caitlin just knew that this was a very special tree. Its trunk was worn and aged through time, but smooth and comforting to the touch. Its winding branches twisted and turned with each leaf singing a soothing melody as the wind gently moved them. Caitlin had never seen a tree quite like this one before, it was magical. Standing underneath its branches it was impossible to feel anything but peace and love. Angels sat underneath the tree talking to children of all nationalities who needed their help.

"This is the Healing Tree" announced Bethan. "Let's find a place to sit down, shall we?"

There was a small area of mossy grass by the tree, "This looks like a good place" said Bethan.

Caitlin sat down with her back against the tree. It felt warm and comforting as if it was reassuring her that everything was going to be alright.

"Bethan" she said "I felt as if the Healing Tree just gave me a hug, but that's silly, trees can't give hugs can they?"

"This is a very powerful tree" replied Bethan. "Nothing that happens here would surprise me.

This tree often gives you a hug when you need one. Most children don't realise it though. You must be a very special little girl to have felt its healing power already!"

"Wow! That's amazing" gasped Caitlin.

"This tree is amazing. The Healing Tree wants all children to be happy. In all the years I have brought children here, the Healing Tree has never ever failed. Now Caitlin, are you sitting comfortably?"

"Yes thank you Bethan, it's so peaceful here."

"Yes it is" said Bethan. "Now Caitlin, I brought you here to help you to see your life from a different perspective; to teach you about optimism and thinking positively. So let's get started, shall we? Do you think you can tell me how you feel about Daddy being ill?"

Caitlin's lip trembled and she began to cry. "I feel sad and angry that MY Dad has got this illness. It's just not fair. Why did it have to be him? Why MY Dad? I don't understand."

"I agree with you" said Bethan "it isn't fair."

Caitlin began to explain, she was totally unaware that all the fairies were listening to her; trying to think of ways that they could help. Infact all the Fairy folk could see what a sweet child she was and they longed to see her radiant smile again.

"Seeing my Dad in so much pain makes me feel sad and helpless, even when he's having a good day he's still in pain. I mustn't be too noisy because my Dad's head hurts so much. Mum said that his brain is a bit like a computer; too much noise or too many things happening around him make his computer crash and shut down. Then he has to go to sleep for his brain to rest and start to work again.

On the bad days Daddy doesn't always understand me properly, it's really hurtful and I get so frustrated. I know it's not his fault and I should have more patience, but it really upsets me" explained Caitlin.

"That must be so difficult for you to cope with" said Bethan.

"It is. It makes me sad that I can't be like other children and I can't talk to my friends about how I feel because they don't understand what it's like.

Dad struggles with noise, so we have to be quieter than most children and he can't go to noisy places with us. He finds it difficult to go to school plays and has never been to a school sports day."

Unbeknown to Caitlin three little fairies were sitting behind her listening to her story with tears in their eyes. "It seems so unfair" they said "Caitlin is such a lovely girl. What can we do? We must think of something to cheer her up."

Meanwhile Caitlin continued…
"I know I really shouldn't, but I can't help feeling jealous when I watch the other children with their Dads on sports day. Most of them take it for granted that their fathers will be there; they don't know how lucky they are."
Bethan gently put her arm around Caitlin's shoulders to comfort her.

"There, there sweetheart, have you been hiding your true feelings from everyone and putting on a brave face?"

Caitlin nodded "Yes, apart from Rufus. He listens to me when he sits on my windowsill at night. I always tell Rufus everything, but I never thought he'd be able to help me. I'm still confused about all that."

"Don't worry sweetheart, all will become clear in time. So what about Chris? Surely he would understand how you feel?" said Bethan.

"Yes, I know he would, but I think Chris has accepted the way things are now, at least it seems that way. He is such a fantastic big brother and I know I'm really lucky to have him. He always looks after me. If I told him how I really felt, then he'd be so worried, and I don't want that" explained Caitlin.

"Well what about your Mum?"

"My Mother works so hard looking after everyone and always puts us first. She tries to compensate for the fact that Daddy's ill and she'd be so sad if I told her how I really feel. Oh Bethan I feel so confused, and guilty for having these feelings. I don't want to feel this way."

"My dear child, your Mum wants you to tell her when you're feeling sad. She's always been honest with you, hasn't she? Right from the beginning she explained how your lives would change, didn't she?"

Caitlin nodded her head as she sniffled "Yes, she has always done her best to explain things so that we would understand, and she's never hidden anything from us."

"Caitlin, if you don't tell her how you're feeling then how can she help you?"

"I know you're right Bethan. I should have talked to my Mum, but I didn't want to worry her" she said wiping her eyes.

"Sweetheart, your Mum worries about you anyway. All parents worry about their children as you'll find out one day when you have children. Your Mum wants to support you as much as she can" explained Bethan.

"I just feel so confused" said Caitlin "I feel sorry for my Dad; being ill all the time must be so hard for him. He gets very grumpy sometimes and has no patience with me and my brother because he's in so much pain. He always says sorry when he's feeling a bit better, but it's really difficult to live with. I hate seeing him in pain, I just feel so useless. I wish there was more I could do to stop him suffering, but there isn't."

As Caitlin finished talking she could hear whispering and giggling behind her. She quickly looked around to see who it was, but there was no one there.

"Did you hear that?" she asked.

Bethan smiled and nodded her head.

"Come with me" she said guiding Caitlin to the far side of the Healing tree.

Caitlin couldn't believe what she saw next. Standing in front of her were three of the fairies she'd seen by the stream earlier. Each one sparkled and glistened from head to toe, as if they were magically glowing.

They smiled at Caitlin as they began to hum a tune that sounded familiar to her. She turned to Bethan "Oh I know that tune, my Mum used to sing that lullaby to me when I couldn't sleep."

"I know sweetheart" said Bethan.

As the fairies got closer and closer they began to dance around Caitlin's feet as they sang the lullaby.

The tune was the same but the words were different....

"Do not cry, do not sigh, our sweet little Caitlin.
You are here in Fairyland to be healed by one and all.
We will help you to see all the good in your life.
You are strong, you are brave and you're LOVED Caitlin dear."

(Sung to Brahms Lullaby)

Bethan glanced over at Caitlin. The tears were rolling down her face, but there was a radiant beaming smile from ear to ear. It was obvious to everyone that she felt overwhelmed by their kindness.

"Oh thank you! That was so beautiful" she said clapping her hands.

The fairies walked over to Caitlin, each giving her a magical woodland flower.

The lilac fairy gave her a lilac flower, so perfect and delicate with tiny silver sparkles that shimmered on each petal. The pink fairy gave her a bright pink flower which looked like a rose and smelled divine. Finally the yellow fairy gave Caitlin the prettiest yellow primrose in the shape of a star and whispered

"You are more perfect than all these flowers. You are strong of mind, kind of heart, clever and wise. You're beautiful both inside and out. Please remember all that you learn today and know that we all love you, precious Caitlin!"

Bethan explained "Because you have opened your heart to me the healing has already started. Did you feel a warm glow inside when the fairies were singing to you?"

"Yes I did" said Caitlin. "It must have been the sun, it's so warm here."

"No dear" smiled Bethan "that was the Healing Tree sending its healing energy to you. As we sit here and talk, it will continue to heal you."

"Wow! Really?"

"Yes Caitlin. The Healing Tree wants you to be happy again. Now I want you to think happy thoughts about your Dad."

"OK, I'll try. Dad takes us out on bike rides when he feels well enough, it isn't very often but at least he makes the effort to take us when he can. Very often he has to go back to bed after the bike ride because he's so tired but he always tells us not to worry, that it was worth it to spend time with us.

Oh I know, we go for little walks in the woodlands near our cottage, which I really enjoy. They aren't like the big adventures that we used to have together, but they're still lots of fun.

Dad used to be a teacher and he helps me with my homework when I get stuck. He explains things so well to me; he is a good teacher.

He has time to listen to us and he encourages us in whatever we're doing.

Even when Dad's ill, he always tells me that I'm his little princess. I know that he loves me and he always gives me lots of hugs and kisses. I love my Daddy so much; I hate him being poorly."

CHAPTER SEVEN

Positive Lessons.

Bethan sat down beside Caitlin and explained,

"Now that your Dad's life has changed he has got lots of time to spend with you and your brother. He couldn't do that when he was working away during the week, could he? He may not be able to do all the things that he could do before, but that's not his fault. He spends quality time with you whenever he feels well enough. He does as much as he can, Caitlin. He probably feels really guilty that he can't be like the other Dads. Did you ever think of it that way? Your Dad didn't ask for this illness, he doesn't want life to change any more than you do, but he's realised that he has to make the best of a bad situation because there's absolutely nothing he can do to change it. Try to remember that every cloud has a silver lining; you just have to look for it. Always hang onto hope, no matter how gloomy things may seem. Do you understand what I'm saying to you?"

"I think so" replied Caitlin. "You're telling me that I should try and make the best of the situation. I should think of what my Dad can do, instead of dwelling on what he can't do anymore. Is that right?"

"Absolutely!" said Bethan putting her arms around Caitlin and hugging her tightly. "You need to focus on what Daddy CAN do now. Think of what is possible on the bad days; even if it's just sitting down quietly with him for 5 minutes and reminding him how much you love him. That would mean the world to him. Tell him about your day; help him to feel a part of your world even when he feels too poorly to be properly involved. You need to step back and think about all the little things in life that pass us by, but if we stop to appreciate them, they make life so much sweeter.

I am so proud of you Caitlin. Now I'm going to teach you a way of staying positive when you start to feel angry or sad, OK?"

"OK" agreed Caitlin.

"This may sound a little strange so I want you to try it with me now. Shut your eyes and picture the journey we made to the Healing tree."

Caitlin shuffled herself to get comfortable before shutting her eyes and remembering the wonderful evening she'd just had.

"When you can picture yourself sitting underneath the tree, I want you to remember what the fairies told you. Concentrate carefully on these words.You are strong of mind, kind of heart, clever and wise, beautiful both inside and out."

As Bethan spoke a warm wind circled the Healing Tree gently blowing Caitlin's hair.

"Now how do you feel Caitlin?" asked Bethan.

"Calm" replied Caitlin.

"Remember what you've learned here sweetheart and in the future when you're feeling upset say to yourself, Let it be. It's no-one's fault. Let it be."

Caitlin opened her eyes in amazement. "Wow, Bethan that really works! I feel so different now. I have hope again and I don't feel sad at all anymore; I feel so happy. Thank you!"

"Just remember what you have learned about being positive sweetheart, and remember that if you let other people know how you feel then they can help you as well."

"Do you mean my Mum?" asked Caitlin.

"Yes, but other people in your life as well" replied

Bethan. "Don't be afraid to show your emotions and let others know how you're feeling. I think you'll be surprised by how many people care about you!"

"Who?" asked Caitlin.

"Your family, friends and schoolteachers; they all want to help you. They'll guide you and support you, if only you'll let them in! Your life may be different from other people's lives; but you can still have a happy life. Most importantly remember that you're never alone! There's always someone to turn to!"

"Thank you so much" said Caitlin putting her arms around Bethan and hugging her tightly.

"I understand now. Thank you for helping me see things differently; I can see that I was being silly trying to hide how I felt. It just made me miserable all the time. Thank you for helping me."

While Caitlin had been talking the fairy folk had been gathering around the Healing tree, behind her just out of sight. They listened intently as she spoke to Bethan, each smiling and nodding their heads knowingly. Some had tears in their eyes, tears of joy and relief that they'd been able to help Caitlin somehow.

Bethan put her hand on Caitlin's shoulder and gently turned her around so she could see the gathering behind her. One by one the fairy folk came up to her to give her a hug. They were genuinely happy for Caitlin as they knew her life would change its course from now on. From this moment onwards she wouldn't be that sad little girl anymore despite her circumstances, she had learned how to look at the situation from a new perspective.

"You've all been so kind to me" said Caitlin. "Until tonight I didn't even believe in fairies…and look at me now! Daddy told me that fairies were real and I should have listened to him instead of thinking I knew better. I will never ever forget this night as long as I live! Thank you all so much; you have been amazing! I don't know how you did it, but I don't feel sad anymore. Now I know that I have the power within me to be happy, I promise I'll try to stay positive from now on."

One by one the fairy folk started to clap until everyone was clapping and cheering for Caitlin.

"Hooray" they cheered as they began dancing and spinning her around till she felt dizzy.

"Ooh you're all spinning a bit too much" said Caitlin laughing "I think I'll have to sit down for a minute."

Bethan took Caitlin's hand and gently sat her down as the fairy folk came and sat beside her. "We're so pleased we could help you" they said.

Bethan continued "You'll do well in life if you remember what you've learned and always stay positive, no matter what life may bring.

Remember you are never alone. You can always call on us for help and guidance.

Remember – When you're down to nothing, God is up to something! It's at times like these that one of the Angels will be sent to help you. We can only bring children to Fairyland though, when you're a grown up the Angels will guide you in other ways. We are always there whenever someone is in need but you may not always realise you have an Angel helping you. Angels are all around us, it might be someone you know or someone who comes into your life just at a time when you need support and leaves when you no longer need them. Just know that we are watching over you and guiding you."

"Wow! That's amazing! Thank you! How can I ever repay you?" asked Caitlin.

"Happiness is all the payment we need. You are such a wonderful child with so many beautiful qualities; don't ever change, not for anyone! Always stay true to yourself. Be yourself and most importantly be happy!" said Bethan.

At last Caitlin was happy. She stretched her arms

and yawned. "Oh Bethan, I don't know why but I feel so tired. Can I just have a little ...."

Before she could finish talking a swirling lilac mist circled the tree in front of her. As the mist cleared it revealed a magical little bed nestled at the foot of the tree. It was just the right size for Caitlin. Its pillow was made out of soft feathers, with a snugly blanket which seemed to be made from leaves woven together. It looked too inviting for Caitlin to resist.

She walked over to the bed, hardly able to keep her eyes open.

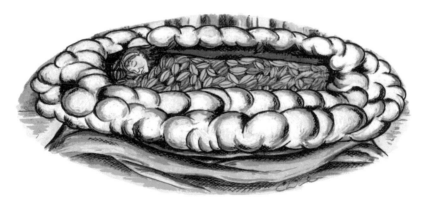

As she climbed into the bed the three fairies began to sing to her again....

"Go to sleep, go to sleep,

Our sweet little Caitlin,
Don't forget us when you wake,
We are always here for you.
We have helped you to see all the good in your
life,
You are strong, you are brave,
And you're loved Caitlin, dear!"

(Sung to Brahms lullaby)

As they sang her eyes became heavier and heavier, until she couldn't keep them open any longer and she drifted into a peaceful sleep. As she dreamed the swirling lilac mist reappeared surrounding her.

Bethan said goodbye to all the fairy folk before gently lifting Caitlin from the bed. As she did the lilac mist began swirling around them both until it lifted them into the air, carrying them safely away from Fairyland, through the starlit night and back to Caitlin's home.

Caitlin remained fast asleep unaware of the fact that she was home again. Bethan carefully placed her back into her own bed, tucked her in snugly and kissed her on the forehead.

"Goodnight sweet Princess" she whispered before vanishing in the blink of an eye. Just as quickly as she had appeared, she was gone.

CHAPTER EIGHT.

Happiness.

As dawn broke and the morning sun glinted through the curtains it woke Caitlin from her deep sleep. She sat up in bed, shook her head and rubbed her eyes.

"Did that really happen?" she wondered.

She didn't know for sure, after all most of her bedtime stories were about Fairies, Pixies and a magical place called Fairyland. So maybe it was all just a dream, or was it?

As she sat there she noticed something very strange. She was dirty! How could that be?

"I had a bath last night" she thought to herself. She climbed out of bed and walked over to the mirror. She was shocked by the reflection that greeted her.

She was wearing a crown! It was made out of ivy and woodland flowers; identical to the ones she'd seen in her dream. Her hair was tangled and matted with leaves in it; her nightdress was covered in dirt, moss and twigs. She looked as if she'd been sitting underneath…a tree!

"It WAS real!" she squealed jumping up and down. She was so excited she felt as if she would burst. She had been to Fairyland. Bethan was real after all, imagine that! An Angel took her to Fairyland! She felt a warm glow inside; an inner peace. She wasn't that sad little girl anymore. "Today is a new beginning" she said to herself. "From now on things are going to be different; I'm going to stay positive no matter what happens!"

She wanted to shout out loud from the rooftops for all to hear "I've been to Fairyland!"

Then she thought "who on earth is going to believe me?"

She decided to go and get herself a glass of water. She needed time to think how she was going to approach this.

Unbeknown to Caitlin, Rufus was sitting on the kitchen windowsill waiting for her. He knew all about her trip to Fairyland; after all he had been the one who'd asked for their help. Something had changed overnight though; from now on their little chats would be very different. Caitlin was about to learn how her visit to Fairyland would change her life forever.

As she walked across the kitchen the morning light gently streamed through the kitchen window creating a magical golden glow across the room.

"Good morning Caitlin. How are you today? You're up early, did you sleep well?" said Rufus chuckling to himself. He knew she'd hardly slept a wink!

Caitlin spun around to look behind her; no-one was there of course. She shook her head in disbelief.

"I'm hearing things" she said.

"Oh no you're not. Look over here by the window. It's me; Rufus!"

"Hello Rufus" she said automatically before realising what she'd done.

"Hang on a minute. This is silly! You're a robin! You can't talk!"

"Oh yes I can! I always could but you couldn't understand me. Only special children who have been to Fairyland can understand the animals and birds."

"Wait a minute, how do you know that I visited Fairyland last night?"

"Well if you hadn't been to Fairyland you wouldn't

be able to understand me, would you? I just told you that!"

Caitlin laughed "Oh yes, so you did! OK you win."

"I don't know what to do Rufus, should I tell my Mum about it all? What if she thinks I've gone mad? Maybe she won't believe me."

"What did Bethan tell you to do?" asked Rufus.

"Hang on a minute, you know Bethan?"

Just then it all became clear in Caitlin's mind; she remembered that she'd been told that all would become clear in time.

"It was you who asked Bethan to help me, wasn't it?"

Rufus looked down at the floor sheepishly "Well I may have mentioned it when I last went to Fairyland… but only because I was so worried about you. You were so sad and I hated seeing you that way. I knew they'd be able to help you!"

Caitlin smiled. She was glad she had such a kind hearted friend to care about her.

"It's OK Rufus, I'm not angry with you at all. Bethan and the fairy folk have helped me so much, how could I possibly be angry? Thank you for caring enough to ask for help."

Rufus looked up at her tilting his head to one side "So you're not angry?"

"No, not at all; thank you! You're so kind."

Rufus hopped closer to Caitlin "I am always here for you, you know that don't you? I will always listen to you and no-one will ever know that I'm actually talking to you. They will only be able to hear a tweeting sound."

Caitlin giggled "That's so cool! It'll be our little secret!"

"That's right" said Rufus. "Now can you remember what Bethan told you to do?"

"Yes" said Caitlin "she said that I should talk to my Mum. Do you think she'll believe me though?"

Rufus thought for a moment before answering. "Maybe not at first, but I'm sure you'll be able to convince her it was real eventually."

Caitlin poured herself a drink. "Would you like something to eat and drink Rufus?"

"Oh yes please, Caitlin. It's freezing cold out here this morning."

She poured a small cup of water for Rufus and put it on the windowsill before opening the door of her Mother's special cupboard where she kept all her best cakes and biscuits. She reached inside and pulled out a large cake tin. As she lifted the lid off, it revealed a large chocolate cake smothered in rich chocolate frosting. Her Mum had baked it the day before as a special treat for Caitlin and Chris.

Anxiously Rufus said "Caitlin, you know that's not the stale cake that your Mum usually gives me."

"I know" she replied mischievously.

"It's a fresh chocolate cake with extra frosting on top and it's going to taste delicious! Today you deserve more than just stale crumbs…you deserve the best, because you're such a wonderful friend."

Rufus gasped. "Won't your Mother be cross?"

"Ah well you see I have a plan! We're going to share it, so that way when I say that I ate the cake, I won't be lying, will I?" she giggled.

"Oh Caitlin you are naughty" said Rufus smiling "but that cake does look very tempting."

So she cut a large slice of cake, putting a small portion of it on her plate and the rest of it on the windowsill for Rufus.

They both ate it quickly before anyone caught them. It was just as well that they did, because 5 minutes later Caitlin's Mother came downstairs and went into the kitchen for breakfast. She was shocked to see Caitlin up so early; she was a child who liked her sleep!

"Good morning sweetheart, you're up early today aren't you? Are you OK?"

Just then she saw the plate with crumbs on it.
"Caitlin!" she scolded. "Did you have chocolate cake for breakfast again? The chocolate cake I made for tonight's dessert?"

She rolled her eyes in despair, trying to remain strict but finding it hard not to laugh. She could see the funny side of it too, after all who would choose cereal for breakfast if they could have double chocolate cake with extra frosting instead? "Caitlin we've talked about this, haven't we?"

"Sorry Mum, but it looked so nice!" Caitlin said

using the puppy dog eyes that she knew her mother could not resist. It always worked and this time was no exception.

"It was really yummy by the way!" she said smiling.

Mum gave in and hugged Caitlin tightly "Well I suppose once won't hurt, but don't do it again!"

At that moment her Mother noticed that Caitlin was dirty and wearing a crown of ivy and flowers. Puzzled she thought to herself "I'm sure Caitlin had a bath last night." She knew something must have happened for her to be in such a state, but decided to broach the subject gently.

"So did you sleep well last night?" she asked.

Caitlin hesitated. She knew that she had to tell her Mum, but didn't know where to start.

"Mum, can I please talk to you?"

"Of course you can sweetheart. What's the matter?" asked her Mother sitting down in the rocking chair. She beckoned for Caitlin to come and sit on her knee.

"All right Princess, what's wrong?"

Caitlin climbed onto her Mother's lap all the time wondering "Am I doing the right thing? Will she think I've gone mad?"

"I really don't know where to begin…" said Caitlin.

"Well let's try at the beginning because that's always a good place to start. I'd love to know where that pretty crown came from; it's so unusual."

Caitlin smiled and sighed with relief, maybe this wasn't going to be so difficult after all.

"You know you asked me if I slept well last night?" she started "Well actually I didn't sleep much at all! Oh Mum, I went on the most amazing adventure last night. You'll never guess! When I went to bed I was feeling really alone. You see none of my friends understand how I feel and it was upsetting me."

"Oh sweetheart" said her Mother holding her close "You're never alone, I'm always here for you."

"Yes, I know that, but it's difficult sometimes because none of my friends understand what my life is like with Dad being ill all the time. I used to let it get me down, but guess what Mum? I won't let it get me down any more! Something happened last night that has changed the way I look at things now."

"Really? That sounds fascinating. What happened?" asked her Mother.

"When I went to bed last night I noticed a bright light in the corner of my room. I didn't know what it was at first, but then it started changing its shape until it turned into a beautiful Angel."
Mum gasped in shock, she didn't expect to hear that! "You saw an Angel?"

"Yes! I'm not joking Mum. It was an Angel! She was so beautiful! She had bright blonde hair which shimmered like gold, piercing deep brown eyes, ruby red lips and the kindest face I've ever seen. Her wings were so white they dazzled me as the light reflected off them and she was just…." Caitlin stuttered as she recalled "she was just amazing. She told me that her name was Bethan and she had been sent to help me. She didn't want me to be sad anymore. She asked me to go with her, and I really wasn't sure Mum. I remembered what you've always told me about not going with strangers, and guess what? She understood. She explained that this was different, and to be honest I had no doubt that she was an Angel. She was glowing from head to toe! She took my hand and away we flew, through the night sky to a place called Fairyland."

"Well Caitlin, it sounds as if you had a wonderful dream last night" replied her Mother.

"But Mum….."

"It must have been a dream if you went to Fairyland. You probably got the idea for your dream from one of your fairy stories; after all you're always reading them, aren't you?"

"Oh but Mum, please listen to me" begged Caitlin. "It wasn't a dream, it really wasn't! At first when I saw Bethan in my bedroom I thought I must be dreaming so I pinched myself hard to see if I was awake. It really hurt and the mark is still there, which proves that it wasn't a dream! I didn't imagine this, honestly!"

"OK well carry on and tell me more about it then" said Mum.

"When we got to Fairyland there were other children there too. Each child had an Angel with them, just like me!
There were pretty fairies that sang to me and danced around to cheer me up. I met real pixies! They were so charming, yet mischievous at the same time, playing hide and seek with each other in the woods…..

Do you know what Mum? They ALL knew my name and who I was! Can you imagine that? Here I was feeling so sad and alone and all along they were there, just waiting to help me! How amazing is that?"

"Hang on a minute. You mean to tell me that Fairyland really exists and that they knew who you were?"

"Yep!" replied Caitlin smiling.

"No, I don't think so my darling. This must have been a very vivid dream. It's quite brilliant, but it's definitely a dream!"

"There's so much more to tell you" Caitlin continued completely ignoring her Mother's disbelief.

"Bethan led me along this magical winding pathway to an old tree in the middle of Fairyland. They call it the Healing Tree and there were children from all over the world sitting underneath the tree talking to their Angels. We both sat underneath the tree just like the others and we talked. The Healing Tree was so mystical; as I leaned against the tree trunk it was healing me and hugging me. It was like nothing I've ever felt before, ever!"

"Now wait a minute Caitlin. You mean to tell me that there was a tree that heals and hugs you? No my dear, that was definitely a dream!" insisted her mother.

Caitlin sighed with frustration; this was proving to be harder than she'd imagined it would be. Determined to make her Mother believe she continued
"It wasn't a dream!"

She thought hard. How was she going to convince her? She looked down at the floor whilst she thought. Then suddenly it came to her…
"Look at me!" she demanded.

"If it was a dream then why did I wake up like this? I'm wearing the fairies' crown on my head and I'm covered in twigs and leaves from sitting underneath the Healing Tree. If this was all a dream then I would still be clean, after all I had a bath last night!"

Her Mother thought about the facts and considered the possibility that her daughter had been sitting under a tree.

"Maybe..." she pondered.

Caitlin didn't waste any time in seizing the opportunity and she continued "But most of all why do I feel so happy now? I know Dad loves me and that he can't help being poorly. Best of all though I know that I'm never alone! I've only got to remember the Healing tree to feel the love and support from all the Fairy folk.
I feel so happy that I suppose it doesn't really matter if no-one believes me.
I know that it was real and I will always remember it as long as I live!"

Her Mother looked closely at Caitlin's face and her radiant smile. She thought to herself "Something has changed within her. I haven't seen her smile like that for a long time. Maybe there could be some truth in all of this. Just maybe it wasn't a dream after all."

She put her arms around Caitlin and gave her a reassuring hug.

"I suppose if you feel so strongly about all this, then maybe it wasn't a dream after all."

Caitlin beamed from ear to ear, hardly able to contain her excitement. Her Mother believed her!

"The most important thing is that you have learned that you're never alone!" Mum said. "There's always someone to turn to whenever you need a shoulder to cry on, or advice. You know you can always talk to me, don't you sweetheart?"

"But you're always so busy looking after Dad, I don't want to bother you" replied Caitlin.

"Sweetheart, I'm your Mother! I love you! I will always make time for you whenever you need me. You can always talk to me, no matter how busy I may seem."

Caitlin squeezed her Mother tightly. She felt relieved to have discussed how she felt at last.
"I love you so much!" she said.
"I love you more!" said Mum smiling. This was a personal joke that they had always shared, each would say "I love you" then they'd say "but I love you more!" in turns until eventually one of them would give up from giggling so much.

"Caitlin you'll never know just how special you are! I am so proud of you! You and your brother have coped brilliantly with all the recent changes in your lives. None of us wanted things to change but they have and there's absolutely nothing we can do about it. I've been impressed with how you've handled it, and maybe because of that I've overlooked how you were feeling deep down. I'm truly sorry Caitlin. I should have paid more attention to you. I'm so sorry that you were feeling so sad and alone. I love you more than words could ever explain. You can always talk to me. Do you understand that now?"

Caitlin hugged her Mum tightly.

"Yes I understand. Please don't feel guilty Mum, it's OK. I should have talked to you, I can see that now. Bethan told me you'd listen and she was right."

Mum smiled and said "I'm so happy that you can see things differently now Caitlin. I'm really proud of you, my little princess."

Later on that same day Caitlin decided to tell her brother Chris all about her adventure. Just like her Mother, Chris found it hard to believe at first, but Caitlin was determined to convince him it had really happened. By the end of their conversation Chris believed her. He found it fascinating, listening carefully to every detail as Caitlin told him what she had learned.

"Maybe I'll be lucky enough to go to Fairyland one day" he said. "It sounds like an amazing place."

"So you believe me?"

"Yes, I do. At first I thought you were teasing me, but as you told me more and more I could see that you were serious. I'm just so glad that Bethan and the fairy folk were able to help you find your lost smile! It's so good to see you happy again. You've got such a pretty smile, sis. You know you can always talk to me if you're ever feeling down, don't you?"
"I didn't want to worry you" replied Caitlin.

"It's OK, you can always turn to me, sis. You're so precious to me, I'd hate to think of you being so sad and keeping your feelings inside. So have we got a deal then? From now on you'll let me help you?"

"OK" agreed Caitlin. "You're the best brother in the whole wide world."

As time went by Caitlin shared more and more of what happened with her brother and instead of teasing her about it, he sat and listened intently. Despite the fact that he had been coping with his father's illness better than his sister, Chris still felt angry about the fact that his Dad had become disabled. He missed the 'old' Dad who was fearlessly adventurous, but he'd felt unable to share these feelings with anyone. As he was naturally a quieter child than Caitlin, people had assumed that he was fine when deep down he wasn't.

He relished having the opportunity to discuss his feelings with Caitlin and she helped him to overcome his bitterness.

They both started to think more positively about their Dad's illness, appreciating every single moment that he spent with them so much more than they had before.

They no longer thought "Why my Dad?"
Instead they thought "Why not my Dad?"

They both realised that disability and illness can affect anyone at anytime. It's no-one's fault. That's just the way life goes sometimes.

A deep rooted change had taken place within Caitlin. That sad little girl was gone forever.

Everybody noticed the difference. She was so positive and happy now, in spite of everything.

Life in the village continued as it always had, apart from one exception. No-one knew that Caitlin had returned from fairyland with a special gift. Not only could she talk to Rufus, but she could understand all the animals and birds, and they could understand her!

She decided that it was best to keep her new

found ability a secret for now. It was just easier that way.

Rufus and Caitlin continued their daily chats but anyone who overheard them would just think that Rufus was tweeting back to Caitlin. We know different though, don't we?

The most important thing of all was that Caitlin's smile was no longer lost; in fact it was never lost again!

It didn't matter what life brought, she could always see the glimmer of hope in it.

Both Chris and Caitlin remained positive throughout their lives thanks to the lessons learned one night in Fairyland.
Caitlin never forgot the Healing Tree or the very special Angel who took her there.

The End

INFORMATION PAGES.....

So what is a Young Carer?

A young carer is a child or young person (aged under 25) who helps in lots of ways to look after someone at home. That person might be an adult or child who has a long-term illness, a disability, a mental health problem or a problem related to drugs or alcohol.

There are many ways to care for somebody. A lot depends on the type of condition that they have. Here are some examples of the type of care they may need.

- Personal Care e.g., Dressing, Washing, Toileting.

- Domestic e.g., Cleaning, Cooking, Laundry

- Emotional Support e.g., Cheering them up when they're down, reassuring them and other family members that everything will be alright and being there for them during the bad times.

- Other day to day tasks can include shopping, paying bills, or looking after your brothers or sisters.

- Helping them or reminding them to take their medication.

- Helping them get about, e.g. Wheelchair

Some young carers may have to do more than others do, but their lives are still affected in both negative and positive ways. Caring for someone can be hard work; at times you may feel sad, angry, tired or even exhausted. Your education can be affected too. You might be late for school, it might be hard to find time to do your homework, and you might miss days because you are tired or the person you are caring for needs someone to stay with them. When you are in school you might not be able to concentrate because you are worrying a lot.

If it is your brother or sister who is unwell, your parents might not have as much time as they'd like to spend with you, you could feel left out. You might not be able to go out as much as your friends. Perhaps you find it hard to make friends because people don't understand what you are going through. Young Carers' Projects offer Young Carers a break from their caring role to meet other young carers who understand. They also provide support, counselling, advocacy, fun trips and activities.

(Source of information – Swansea, Neath Port Talbot Crossroads Young Carers Project, Wales, UK)

Young Carers' Support. (UK only)

Young Carers.net
http://www.youngcarers.net/

Princess Royal Trust for Carers
http://www.carers.org/

Crossroads Care
www.crossroads.org.uk

Barnardo's
www.barnardos.org.uk

Children's Society
http://www.childrenssociety.org.uk/

Action for children
http://www.actionforchildren.org.uk

For schools –

The Princess Royal Trust for Carers and The Children's Society's

'Schools resource pack'

http://professionals.carers.org/young-carers/articles/schools-resource-pack,6282,PR.html

This resource helps schools identify and support Young Carers, and includes many time saving tools.

(It is a free to download resource for any school to use.)

So what is IH?

IH is an invisible illness where the person looks "fine" when they are not!

That is why I am taking this opportunity to help raise awareness for IH and the Intracranial Hypertension Research Foundation (IHRF), which is working hard to improve the lives of people affected by IH.

"Intracranial hypertension" literally means that cerebrospinal fluid (CSF) pressure within the skull is too high. Chronic intracranial hypertension (IH) is a serious neurological disorder that can cause severe headaches, vision loss, blindness and life-altering disability.

Anyone can develop chronic IH at anytime in life.
There currently is no cure.

Old names for IH include Pseudotumour Cerebri and

Benign Intracranial Hypertension. Most people have never heard of it, including many in the medical profession. If more people knew about IH, then patients might get treated with the compassion they deserve!

IH is sometimes caused by an existing medical condition, but it often occurs without a known cause. Idiopathic IH (IH that occurs without a cause) is considered a rare illness affecting 1 in 100,000, though the rate of incidence is as high as 1 in 5000 for some people.

Millions of other people have a condition or disease such as traumatic brain injury, stroke or kidney failure, in which IH can play a role.

There has never been a drug specifically developed to treat IH. Treatment options are limited. For some people, medication can help control intracranial pressure. But for others, the only choice is painful surgery to insert a shunt to drain the excess fluid from the brain. Since shunt surgery only has a 50% success rate, this frequently means many surgeries, with the accompanying risks. If sight is at risk, a person with IH often has to undergo optic nerve surgery to save their vision.

IH symptoms include:

Severe headaches (as if your head is in a vice)
Vision loss and / or blindness,

Optic nerve swelling,

Pulse – synchronous tinnitus,

Sore/ stiff neck,

Back pain,

Memory/ cognitive problems,

Fatigue,

Malaise,

Dizziness,

Light-headedness,

Photophobia,

Noise sensitivity.

Chronic IH is life-altering, and robs people of their once happy and healthy existence.

No two cases are the same, making it a difficult condition to manage.

For more information on IH,
Please go to the IHRF's website

http://www.ihrfoundation.org

Source of Information – IH Research foundation.

Thank you for taking the time to read this information!

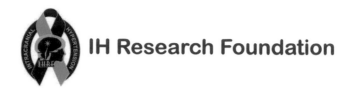 # IH Research Foundation

The IH Research Foundation is the only non profit organisation in the world devoted to supporting and funding the medical research of chronic IH. Their mission is to discover why IH happens, along with new, effective therapies to treat the disorder.
Their ultimate goal is to find a cure.

 # Crossroads Care

Crossroads Care is Britain's leading provider of support for carers and the people they care for. We work with more than 41,000 individuals and their families, helping carers make a life of their own outside caring. We provide flexible services to people of all ages and with a range of disabilities and health conditions.

The IH Research Foundation and Crossroads Care benefit from a percentage of the royalties from all book sales. *

Acknowledgements

To my Husband. We didn't know what lay ahead of us all those years ago when we got married. It's been a difficult journey, but it's made us stronger. IH has changed so many things in our lives, but it'll never change my love for you. Your courage inspires me to help the IHRF as much as I possibly can in their quest to support IH sufferers and one day find a cure.

To Christopher and Adele-Caitlin. You are my inspiration! You are such caring, wonderful people and I'm honoured to be your Mother. You've had to deal with so many difficulties from a young age, yet each time you have shown compassion and maturity. I am so proud of you both. Thank you for being you. I love you!

To all my family and friends. Thank you for always being there and for your continuous love and support. You have given me the strength to carry on when life has been so difficult. Thank you from the bottom of my heart!

To Paul. Thank you for your continuous support with the Caitlin's Wish website and the fantastic publicity photos.
www.phrphotography.com

To Claire. Thank you for being such a good friend and for agreeing to be the Illustrator for Caitlin's Wish. The illustrations are perfect, Thank you!

To. Crossroads Care. Thank you for all that you do for carers. You are a lifeline to so many! A HUGE Thank you to the Young carers project; you've brought light back into my children's world by enabling them to befriend other young carers and just be kids! **www.crossroads.org.uk**

To IH Research Fdtn. Thank you for all that you're doing to educate people about IH, and your efforts to find better treatments and a cure. Thank you for all the advice and information on your website; it really helped us learn about IH. Thank you so much for your continued support, you've helped us so much and we're very grateful! **www.ihrfoundation.org**

To anyone affected by IH. Keep spreading awareness of IH! Together we CAN make a difference! Every case of IH is different BUT the common denominator amongst you all is the courage and strength of character that you all have in dealing with this cruel, painful and disabling condition. I'll continue working hard to raise awareness for IH, I promise! I want to say a special Thank you to the IH patients who reviewed the Second Edition for us.
THANK YOU!

To Young Carers. You are all heroes in my eyes! Thank you for all that you do caring for loved ones, I know it isn't easy and life can be really tough sometimes, but your dedication doesn't go unnoticed! You are amazing young people, and I wanted to take this opportunity to say THANK YOU!

I want to say a special Thank you to the Young Carers who reviewed the Second Edition for us. THANK YOU!

Thank you to **Emanuel Tanne, M.D. Co-Founder and President of the Intracranial Hypertension Research Foundation, Angela Roberts, Director of Wales Crossroads Care, Mr.** Karl Napieralla, **Director of Education for Neath, Port Talbot, Wales, UK, Neath Port Talbot Young Carer's' Forum, Wales, UK and Sonia Binge, Children with Disabilities service, Berkshire, England, UK** for endorsing Caitlin's Wish. Your support means so much to us, Thank you!

I want to say a huge thank you to everyone who has supported 'Caitlin's Wish' since we published the First Edition at the beginning of 2010.

The response we've had has been overwhelming, and you've been so kind.
Thank you!

For all the latest information,
Please go to the
Caitlin's Wish website

www.caitlinswish.co.uk

You can also find us on
Facebook